IT'S A FALOODA OF EMOTIONS

AF094690

VINI KUNHAPPAN

Copyright © Vini Kunhappan
All Rights Reserved.

ISBN 978-1-63920-447-2

This book has been published with all efforts taken to make the material error-free after the consent of the author. However, the author and the publisher do not assume and hereby disclaim any liability to any party for any loss, damage, or disruption caused by errors or omissions, whether such errors or omissions result from negligence, accident, or any other cause.

While every effort has been made to avoid any mistake or omission, this publication is being sold on the condition and understanding that neither the author nor the publishers or printers would be liable in any manner to any person by reason of any mistake or omission in this publication or for any action taken or omitted to be taken or advice rendered or accepted on the basis of this work. For any defect in printing or binding the publishers will be liable only to replace the defective copy by another copy of this work then available.

My loving brother Vicky Kunhappan whom I lost on September 15, 2019.

It's been hard since he left. He has always been my inspiration, always had my back. I owe all my achievements to him. He always stood rock solid for me. As caring and loving he was and typically brotherly annoying too. Eight years older to me, he was almost like a father figure. I don't remember if he had ever missed any of my competitions, recitals, PTM. He was present all along. He was my pillar of strength and continues to guide me from the heavens above.

Bhaiya, I miss you so much.

Dedicating this book to you is nothing compared to what you have done for me. My life will always be indebted to you. Thank you for everything, Bhaiya.

Contents

Acknowledgements	*vii*
1. The Heir	1
2. Not Any Less	5
3. The Regret	9
4. But He Was A Friend	13
5. The Diary	17
6. The Classroom	19
7. Yoga Class	23
8. The Wait	26
9. A Second Chance	29
10. The Story Teller	33
11. The Promise	36
12. The Decision	40
About The Author	43
About Writefluence	45

Acknowledgements

First of all, I would like to thank WriteFluence for providing me with this opportunity.

I would like to thank my dear Parents (R.I.P) because they are the reason for my writings. Pallavi Gawai and Shubhangi Chati for their literary advice. Seema Singh, Kulvinder Saini for always being supportive. My colleagues who, no matter what, have always tried to provide me with their positive inputs. Some of my friends from school, college and B.Ed. thank you for bearing me. They know who they are. Lastly Vishal Singh who always encouraged me to put down my thoughts and who never lost faith in me.

ONE

THE HEIR

It was raining heavily. Savita was in a lot of pain. It was her eighth pregnancy. All the expectation of an heir for the family had led to the birth of seven beautiful daughters. Savita loved them all but her father in law was very particular and wanted a boy. Her father in law or as the villagers called zamindar saheb landlord was a cruel and feared man. She and her husband Sukumar along with her children were thrown out of the biggest house in the village for not providing an heir. And were asked to return only when they had a boy. She was in labour and alone at home. The thunderstorm outside was no match to the pain she was enduring. All while between wincing in pain, her only wish was to have a boy.

After 12 hours of labour and some help from the neighbours at the crackling of dawn she heard the sweetest voice a baby cry.. Yes it was a boy. The entire village was happy. Savita was content and emotional at the same time. She took the baby boy in her hands and knew he would turn this family fortune. Her years of being called names for not producing an heir was finally over. To her surprise the next day her father in law visited her. He didn't even look at

Savita and straight went to the cradle, picked up the baby and in a harsh tone asked them to return home. Savita and her husband Sukumar both ecstatic that finally they will move away from their misery. The household is in a state of merry making. The entire village was in a celebratory mode. The celebrations went on for weeks. As the boy grew he was named Rajan. He was the apple of his grandfather's eyes. He was so attached to his grandfather that he hardly spent time with his parents. For he was turning out to be as arrogant,cruel and feared after like his grandfather. Nobody could say no to Rajan in the village. Whatever he said was done. Even the school where he studied, the principal and teachers feared the wrath of his grandfather hence Rajan always got his way. Rajan on the other hand loved books though that was something that his mother admired in him. She didn't want him to be a zamindar but a person with a good soul and heart. She didn't wanted to raise a devil in the name of an heir. So before things got out of hand . Savita decided to take matters into her own hands. One day out of the blue, she planned a small trip outside the village with her son. Now when they were travelling Rajan noticed a lot of things on the way. Like children playing aimlessly on the road,houses without proper roofs, families without food or clothes. He was so curious as to where his mother was taking him. But Savita didn't utter a word. They just travelled in their bullock cart. As their ride slowed down. Rajan observed a house with mud walls and plastic sheet roof and broken stairs.

Finally his mother asked him to observe the house. He looked all around. It was a little dilapidated house. He wondered who could have stayed here and why his mother was so keen that he saw this. His mother finally broke the silence and told him that he, Rajan was born in this very place. Rajan was shocked surprised at the same time. She told him how she and his father had to move out on the behest of his grandfather for not producing a boy. Rajan was damn furious on his grandfather for treating his parents in such an inhuman manner. But Savita calmed her son down. She explained him that she did not wanted him to hate his grandfather,but try to make use of name,time,education,and resources for the welfare of the people. Years and years the villagers have suffered the atrocities of this family. She wanted him to bring about change. She does not want him to grow up to be a man just like his ancestors. She reminded Rajan to be a leader who people look upon and not a dominant king who people fear. All these words had an immense impact on Rajan. His mother also reminded that money and power will go but your good deeds will always remain.Once they returned back home and as days passed. His behavior had drastically changed. He was now more calm and composed. Rajan after completing his intermediate ,started working for uplifting his village. From wells to hand pumps. From including women in the labour force to women education. From kerosene lamps to electricity in every home.

He made sure everything he does helps his people to prosper. His parents were so happy with his achievements. Although his grandfather didn't agree with his ways of wasting family wealth, but he was getting good returns for the same and a good name to add to that. So he swallowed his pride and suppressed his displeasure. Rajan was happily made the youngest sarpanch of the gram panchayat. A new feat for an old tradition, Rajan's popularity increased so much that even the state took notice. Now it's heard that Rajan is going to contest for the upcoming elections. From a rowdy, cruel arrogant boy to humble caring and people person Rajan has definitely come a long way. God has answered his mother's prayers for sure.

TWO
NOT ANY LESS

Jaanki, lovingly called jaanu by her father, was a different girl. She was the elder of the two daughters. Mahadevji her father, a simple security guard in the railway police, loved his daughters unconditionally. But on the other hand the same could not be said about her mother Meenabai. Who always wanted a son. Jaanki's mother was so much into having a son that she had left no stone unturned. From temples to churches, to mosques to priests,pandits she had tried everything to bore a son but in vain. She even contemplated getting Mahadevji married the second time so the family can have an heir. But her husband loved his wife and children so much that he wouldn't think of a second woman in his life. He treated Jaanki like a boy. Even Jaanki was not your typical girl.

When everyone in her family used tobacco to brush their teeth. She would save up enough pocket money to buy colgate tooth powder. When other girls of her age were learning how to knit and cook, she was riding bicycles with the speed of wind. She was mischievous as hell. Her household used to get two bottles of milk everyday. Jaanki used to sneak one bottle, drink more than half of it and then fill the rest with water and keep it back at its place. Once one of the colony boys punctured her cycle. Jaanki without a thought beat the hell out of him. Her father was quite proud of how Jaanki handled things but on the other hand her mother was pretty embarrassed. She punished Jaanki for no fault of her' but this didn't deter her but made her even more bold. Her mother's need for a boy always made Jaanki give her best at everything.

She was excellent in school. Sports was something she enjoyed a lot. Even the neighbours would tell Meenabai as for who would marry Jaanki as she used to be on practice grounds more often and less at home. Her relatives always talked behind her back and filled her mother's ears with false stories about her daughter. Jaanki who was aware of this never let it stop her from doing what she wanted. She wanted to study and earn good so that she could provide the best of the things to her family. Her father's income although not that much but was sufficient enough for the four of them. As Jaanki graduated with a gold medal in history, instead of being overjoyed her mother was worried about the dowry for her marriage as she had already started looking for some suitable prospects. Jaanki was ready to get married but her only condition was that her parents move in with her or if not she would be taking care of her parents even after her marriage as her future husband would too for his parents. This thought was rejected by most families who came to see her. Her mother too was not happy with this condition. Their relatives were no less always taunting and demeaning Jaanki for her choices.

Nevertheless Jaanki was a determined girl. She knew what she wanted from life: a good job, a better house and all the luxury that money can buy for her parents. Her father was supportive of her choices but it was hard to convince her mother. Life had something else in store for Jaanki. Her uncle (mama) Dev who had an eye on Jaanki for a very long time, would always try to persuade her. In her community it was acceptable to be married to the mother's brother.Jaanki always respected him and never looked up to him as a husband but more of a father figure. Dev on the other hand was weaving dreams of getting married to his own niece.

So to make his dreams come true he started poisoning his own sister's mind, by putting thoughts like how independent her daughter has become in this world she needs a man to control her. Meenabai was literally convinced with these regressive thoughts. He also convinced his own sister to get him married to her daughter. When Jaanki was notified regarding the same. She said no to the proposal and told her parents that she can't marry her own uncle. The thought of it makes her cringe. This rejection didn't go down well with Dev. He felt insulted and felt humiliated on being rejected at the hands of a woman and that to his niece. She was so furious that he wanted to avenge his insult. He was so blinded by his own ego that he hatched a plan to get back at Jaanki. As days went by Jaanki forgot all about it.

One fine afternoon when nobody was at home and Jaanki was resting. She heard a knock, on seeing through the eye view she saw her uncle Dev. She let him in without a second thought. As she was making tea for her uncle, Dev grabbed and started touching her inappropriately. She on the other hand tried to defend her in every way possible.Dev was a strong man and he wanted to make sure that the society humiliates Jaanki. He wanted to make sure that she wouldn't be able to face anyone. With these evil thoughts he just wanted to disrobe her, and prove his masculinity. When he pinned her down to get on with his heinous act, a loud thud moved him.

Dev turned around just to see his sister standing there looking furious. He on the other hand blamed it on Jaanki trying to convince his sister that Jaanki was trying to seduce him. Meenabai no matter how she was, for the first time didn't favour him over his daughter. She choose to side with Jaanki which shocked both Jaanki and Dev. She warned her brother not to be seen at a distance of even hundred yards from her daughter or she wouldn't hesitate killing her own brother. At this Jaanki ran to her mother and hugged her and wept. Meenabai on the other hand tried to console her daughter and apologized for not understanding her all these years. Now years later Meenabai lives in her posh bungalow in the most high facility kitchen cooking for her daughter, looks outside the window to see her daughter Jaanki arrive in a red beacon car for lunch. Jaanki now an IAS officer was the pride of her parents. Meenabai even if late realized that it is not important to have a son, and daughters are equally capable.

THREE
THE REGRET

When Ajinkya tried to open the door to his house, the lock was undone but he couldn't push away the door. He was back from London after two whole years. Somehow he applied all his strength and with great difficulty it did open, onto a pile of letters scattered in the corridor. He picked up one of the letters addressed to him with love Fiona. Ajinkya was dumb struck. He didn't know how to react. His body went numb and his eyes watered. He picked each letter carefully and kept it on his table. Went over to his balcony and pulled away the curtains, his eyes shut tight with the piercing sunlight.

His thoughts: "Why would Fiona write to me? Didn't we separate with mutual consent?"

He wanted to open the letters yet worried with the contents. So he tried to divert himself with a nap, gorging food and watching t.v. And whatnot, the letters kept haunting him the entire day lying on that table giving him a feeling as if they wanted to say something. So after fiddling with the thoughts of whether to read or not, he picked up the bunch of letters and started going through the dates. The last date seemed to be a month ago. He wondered what must be written in it. He gathered up all his courage and opened it. Upon reading it he realized what a terrible decision he had taken two years back. Ajinkya kept the letter aside and recalled his last conversation with Fiona two years ago.

Fiona: Ajinkya we have to get married or my father will get me married to someone I don't love.

Ajinkya: Fiona I have a career to build. I can't take the responsibility of a marriage now. And on top of that our religion and cultures are different. My family will have a hard time accepting you.

Fiona: So are you saying that i should forget these three years and move on. Didn't we decide to be together in the first place?

Ajinkya: Fiona I love you. But I can't marry now. I have got a big opportunity in London and will have to give a couple of years before I could convince my parents and come to your parents to ask for your hand.

Fiona: How long is that going to be?

Ajinkya: A year maybe two, maybe more. Who can tell?

Fiona: My father has given me an ultimatum either you ask for my hand or I have to get married according to his choice. Why don't you understand?

Ajinkya: I can't do anything either you can wait or you can marry wherever your father tells you.

Fiona: Fine then if the choice has to be mine. I will send you an invitation. Please do not try to contact me ever again.

Ajinkya could see the tears in her eyes but was also shocked at her decision. He wanted to stop her but his male ego prevented him from doing so. As he couldn't imagine Fiona choosing anybody else over him.

Now he is back from London with a letter of Fiona in his

hand, and tears in his eyes. He got up and searched through his cupboard. Opened a small phone diary and flipped through its pages. He read one number, picked up his phone and dialed it. The phone rings and somebody picks up from the other side

Ajinkya: Hello this is Ajinkya. Can I talk to Fiona?

An elderly voice: Fiona had told me you would call. How are you Ajinkya?

Ajinkya: I'm fine , who is this? Can i talk to Fiona?

Elderly voice: Fiona is no more. She succumbed to cancer a month ago.

Ajinkya was shocked, he couldn't contemplate what he just heard.

Elderly voice: Ajinkya are you there ? Are you ok.?

Ajinkya: Yeah...hhhhh Im ok..

Elderly voice: I'm Fiona's father. Can you do me a favour? Please come down to my place. I have something that belongs to you.

Ajinkya:Yes, I know I will be there Tomorrow.

Once they hung up. Ajinkya couldn't sleep; he was just waiting for the sun to rise. As soon it was morning he got ready and left for Fiona's place. He was greeted by a very old gentleman, Fiona's father. He welcomed Ajinkya, served him tea and snacks and after all the pleasantries.

Ajinkya: Where is my daughter?

Fiona's father: She is in her bedroom.

They both move towards the bedroom, a small toddler sleeping in her cradle peacefully. Ajinkya picked up the child and hugged it.

Fiona's Father: Once she realised that she was pregnant. She cancelled the wedding and tried to reach out to you. She didn't give up on you. She waited for you till her last breath.

Ajinkya: Im sorry. I couldn't be there with her. I just can't imagine what she must have endured.

Fiona's father: Now that you are here take good care of your daughter. She was very precious to Fiona.

Ajinkya: What shall I call her?

Fiona's Father: Fiona already named her Divya. If you want to change, it's fine.

Ajinkya: No, it's just perfect.

He carries his little bundle of joy with pride and looking up at the sky he promises Fiona to be the best father he can.

FOUR
BUT HE WAS A FRIEND

"Hi I'm the new physics teacher" he said

"Oh! Hello.. Hi my name is Sanjana and I'm a primary teacher here. What's your good name?"

"Well I'm Razak. New to the city, me and my parents just shifted here. What about you??

"Well I was born and brought up here in the city", said sanjana

"Well that's great then you can show me around, well if your husband has no problems, how many kids do you have?", asked Razak

"Hahahahaha (laughing out loudly) I'm sure my husband will have no problem." said sanjana

"Really? Why is that?" asked razak

"Well i don't have one" said sanjana

They both laughed aloud. So loud that the entire staff canteen had their eyes on them.

As days went by they really became good friends at work. Hanging out in the newly opened restaurant to go out for the latest movie. They hit it off very well. So much so that their friendship was the talk of envy for everyone at the workplace.

Razak: Do you drink?

Sanjana: Yes, sometimes,

Razak: vodka?

Sanjana : Ya, but I prefer Whisky or rum more.

Razak: seriously?

Sanjana: Why? Do you?

Razak: Yes, I do.

Sanjana: But your religion does not permit it.

Razak: So does yours and besides I'm an atheist

Sanjana: Wow! That's new for me.

Razak: Let's have a drinking party and binge watch Batman this weekend.

Sanjana:Sounds like a plan. I'm in.

Razak: Whisky here we come.

Both of them giggle and retire to their work.

The weekend party was enjoyed by both as it was joined by two of razak's batch mates and one of Sanjana's close friends. After the party Razak offered Sanjana to drop home. Sanjana agreed. As Sanjana got into the car with Razak she put on the music half drunk she sang her heart out. In the meanwhile Razak who was silent quietly slid his hand on Sanjan's thigh. For a moment sanjana froze in her seat. It was unexpected of Razak to do this. Since Sanjana didn't resist he held her hand and tried to make her touch his crotch. This time Sanjana resisted.

Sanjana(shouting): What are you doing?

Razak: Please touch it. Just once.I want you to touch it

Sanjana: Are you crazy ? What's got into you? How can you do this ? Stop the car... I want to get down.

Razak: I feel like doing it. just touch it once (trying to grab her hand)

Sanjana slaps him. Razak felt quite for a while. He drops her home and leaves. The weekend goes by as Sanjana tries to forget what happened by brushing it as a behaviour due to the influence of alcohol. Both return to work after the weekend only to be talked by the staff in hush hush tones. Sanjana distanced herself from Razak who was roaming the corridors of the building like he had some victory. When Sanjana came to know of it, the pictures of her weekend party with Razak and his friends were all over facebook. One of Razak's friends had tagged each one of them and now it was visible to all present on her friend list. Razak on the other hand started spreading rumours that Sanjana was after him. When Sanjana confronted him.

Sanjana: What is wrong with? When was I after you?

Razak: That's what happens baby when you say no to me.

Sanjana: I thought you were my friend? How could you do this?

Razak: Im not your friend and there is more to come.

Sanjana on the other hand could not go and complain as the incident she was about to narrate did not happen in the school premises. Besides everyone believed Razak. Everybody was like, Sanjana asked for it. Nobody stood by Sanjana as she was single and naive as not to understand that he just wanted to be popular in the school and Sanjana was just a pawn. Sanjana was deeply hurt by the behavioural changes in her staff towards her. Even her bestie didn't believe her.

Sanjana resigned. A few months later Razak made headlines for molesting a fifteen year old girl from school. He was arrested. That's when the people who blamed Sanjana actually believed her. She started receiving calls from her former colleagues to apologize.But Sanjana didn't respond to any. She was just happy that the truth was out.

FIVE

THE DIARY

May 5th1996,
"Dear diary,

You're the only friend I've had all my life. I have shared my dreams,my sorrows,happiness and secret thoughts with you. You know what ,yesterday night i had a dream. I was walking amongst the clouds with unicorns running around. I was so close to the sun but it didn't hurt my eyes. Guess what, there were pretty beautiful angels who welcomed me there. They had beautiful white gowns and shiny wings with star studded tiaras and magic wands. They told me I could ask them for anything. When I enquired what is this place all about ? They said that it's heaven and you will get here all that you like. I was so excited to explore. So as I started looking around I saw rainbow bridges which connected one cloud to the other. There they had chocolate studded trees. Like fruits I did pluck a few. It was delicious. I haven't eaten something like that before. They had pancake shrubs and gummy bear flowers. They were sweet and chewy. The best part was they also had a river filled with chocolate milk just like how mommy makes it.

You won't believe that I even got to ride an unicorn. It was so much fun. The mountains here are made of multiple flavours of pineapple,butterscotch,choc chip and what not. I know I'm not allowed to eat all this but one day cheating won't harm right. You know dear diary I have troubled my parents a lot. I know since the day I was born till the time I was detected with cancer. It's been hard on them. I want to help them out . But can't even stand properly without their help. The chemotherapy kills you literally. The pain is unbearable. But I try to put up a strong face. It's ok, I try my best for them. I'm just a burden and I know it.. It's heart wrenching to see my parents struggle so much just to keep me alive. They have financial issues but they won't discuss them with me. Even though i'm very much aware of it. If this dream of mine is true.

Then dying won't be such a bad idea after all. Yes, I'm scared. In case death brings some relief to my family. I will be happy. I know mom will cry a lot and dad will not be the same again. They will survive. I love them a lot and will continue to do even if I'm not with them. My little sister who is just a baby now won't even remember me once I'm gone. Because she is just a baby . But I will always love her. She is the only person who brings a smile to my face. Hope she keeps smiling always. Dear diary, I'm really tired. I don't think I can write much now."

As her mother closed the diary, her eyes were filled with tears. It was the last entry her daughter had made. She was gone the next day 6 May 1996. To be among the fluffy clouds and riding with the unicorns.

SIX

THE CLASSROOM

The bell rang and students ran out of their class to their buses and parents. It was the last day of the exams and the summer vacation was about to begin. Within minutes the school building stood silent. somewhere in one of the classrooms a bench creaked.

BENCH1: Finally the little devils are off to vacation. I can have a peaceful one month without having to carry someone's butt.

BENCH2 (weeping): I will miss my owner. She was such a dainty girl. Always made sure I was clean and never dropped her food while eating. She always used a table cloth before she started eating

Duster (with a sigh of relief): Oh! You know how relieved I'm, that math teacher Mrs sharmani always takes aim using me to hit students. Did she ever realise how much that hurts me?? No, and she used to rub me against the board like a bar of soap who removes stains. I wish not to see her in the next session.

Teacher' Table(giggling): But i know you have a crush on that English teacher.Mrs.Shaina Isn't it? She seems to be very gentle on you.

Duster(all blushing): Even the students love her.

All benches(in chorus): Duster is in love! Duster is in love!!

Duster(all red in cheeks): Stop it guys!!

Whiteboard: I don't know about you but i love it when the art teacher Mr. Kurshid comes to the class and fills my Life less white self full of vibrant colors. It gives me life again

Soft board (cringing): What would you know white board you are lucky. Look at me. I'm pinned and stapled everywhere. Nobody cares about the pain I endure to make this class look beautiful. Thankless humans.

Bench3: Don't you forget soft board these little brats stand on me to get to you. How mercilessly they stamp on me. You can't imagine. Literally breaking my spine.

Classroom door: Please don't forget me. They bang me on the wall so hard almost shattering my bones while they come running back from their physical education class.

Teachers table: You remember guys how our sangeet samrat Mr. Surmai Sir over crowded me with his instruments and suffocated me.

Bench4: And those extremely painful to the ears songs

All laughed..

Duster: Why haven't they come out to clean us today?

Bench5: I heard some emergency. All were asked to vacate immediately. Something serious has happened out there.

Bench1: The helper is a lazy guy. He doesn't even clean us properly. Most of the time he is talking to his girlfriend on his phone.

Bench4: Ya sometimes he forgets to brush us or mop. He is a forgetful guy

Teacher's table: His partner is no good either. She always chews tobacco, I feel like vomiting when I see her stained teeth. Yucks!!!

Whiteboard: She does rinse me once in a while with water and does bring my shine. So I'm cool.

Bench2: Did you observe the science teacher Miss. Veronica?

(All in chorus "yes")

She was all dressed up. Did I miss something?

Duster: Oh!! I know I heard she got engaged. Soon she will be Mrs. Veronica.

The days went by and a couple of days later some guys showed up in masks and sprayers and started spraying some liquid in the classrooms.

Bench6: What was that? We all are smelling like the sanitizers which the students bring.

Bench5: and see they are locking the door and windows as well. Something is seriously wrong.

Class Cupboard(the wise one): There is something called a corona called a pandemic breakout . I have come to know that it's a deadly virus which is putting the humans at risk.

Bench1: I have heard that too. Humans are under lockdown you see.

Bench3: Yes, it's expected to last 15- 20 days to avoid spreading.

Duster: I just wish nothing would happen to Mrs.Shaina.

Bench4: oh! You pathetic Romeo.

Bench3: Cupboard how did you know all this?

Class Cupboard: I'm filled with a lot of information and secrets. Humans trust me with their important documents. So keeping myself updated is important.

Bench6: Please stop bragging!!

Class cupboard: I'm not bragging. , I'm just wise.

As days went by and summer vacation was over still there was no sign of students

ClassCupboard: Have you heard guys all schools are shut now. Every school is conducting online classes.
Bench2: What does that mean??
Class Cupboard : It means that students won't be coming to class. Till the pandemic is over.
Soft board: And when it will be over?
Class cupboard: I guess once when the lockdown is over.

Days changed into months and months changed into a whole year. Yet the school didn't see a single sign of life. All the tables, chairs, benches had accumulated a thick inch of dust on them. Each nook and corner was waiting for a human to show up. The corridors bore an empty look. The playgrounds were still. Every window pane seemed deadly with a silent look that killed.

Class cupboard: Hey guys just heard something new
Everyone in the room was curious to know.
Class cupboard: I heard the humans have come up with a vaccine to curb this monster called corona.
Teachers table: What a good news in months.
Bench1: Wow!!! So it's back to school again
Bench2 : Im looking forward to see all my little ones
Duster: I hope Shaina takes the shot
Whiteboard : Hmmm Shaina??? From Mrs.Shaina

All laughed after months.

Class table: Lets hope for the best guys. Hope that things come back to normal and this phase of our life never repeats again.

Let's hope for the best, they all chorused.

SEVEN

YOGA CLASS

Juhi was her chirpy self as usual. She was in grade 3 and to her excitement she was having her summer vacation. One month of all fun play and games. She was excited to be with her cousin sister Mahek with whom she would play all day long. Her mother was a yoga freak. Every afternoon Juhi would accompany her mother to the community centre for her yoga classes. The class was on the first floor of the building. Juhi used to get really bored sometimes doing all the asanas. She was good at it and the yoga teacher Mrs.Tripathi always made Juhi her muse as she was small,flexible and shouldn't feel left out amongst adults. There used to be an old watchman to guard that building. Juhi would always get a chocolate from that old fellow. She used to call him kaka(uncle). Sometimes when she was not in the mood for yoga kaka was someone she would play hide-n-seek with.One day when Juhi and her mother were returning back Juhi was very quite. This was not the usual thing.

Mother: What happened Juhi? Are you tired??
Juhi:Nothing mom.

On reaching home Juhi declared she won't accompany her to her yoga classes.

Mother: Why dear? What's wrong?

Juhi: Mom I don't like it there.

The way Juhi was saying things it tweaked her mother's curiosity. Next day her mother decided not to go to the yoga centre. She spent the entire day with Juhi. Cooking her favourite meals and trying to cheer her up. As she wanted to spend more time with her daughter she decided to skip her yoga classes for sometime and take Juhi to her favourite places. Juhi would be happy but something was amiss and Juhi's mother who loved her unconditionally was trying to figure it out. After ten days or so Juhi's mother received a call from her yoga instructor Mrs.Tripathi.

Mrs. Tripathi: Hello ..

Juhi's Mother: Hello Mrs.Tripathi, How are you?

MrsTripathi: I'm good, How are you ? Haven't seen in class for long

Juhi's Mother: Oh! Juhi was not well and I also wanted to spend some time with her. After all, it's her vacation. Once it's over I would hardly get some quality time with her.

Mrs Tripathi: That's true. and how fast they grow up. Time flies for sure

Juhi's Mother: Yes it does

Mrs. Tripathi: Have you heard the news.?

Juhi's Mother: What news??

MrsTripathi: You know that old guy, that watchman.?

Juhi's Mother: Yes, I do,

Mrs Tripathi: That guy got arrested yesterday.The centre has thrown him out of his job.

Juhi's Mother: Why? What happened?

Mrs Tripathi: One of my students couldn't find her daughter after her yoga session. So we all started looking for her frantically. And she ended up finding her daughter in the watchman's cottage who was trying to molest her.

Juhi's mother was shocked. She couldn't contemplate what she had just heard.

MrsTripathi: Who would have thought such an old man would end up doing such a heinous act.

Mother: Mrs.Tripathi I will call you later.

She hung up the phone and went straight to Juhi's room who was playing with her dolls. She saw all her dolls' clothes were removed and they were lying on the floor. Juhi's mother had tears in her eyes. She hugged her daughter tightly.

Juhi's Mother : Why didn't you tell me beta? You should have told me, You should have told me

She kept repeating. On some coaxing Juhi finally revealed what happened that day. She told her mother how on pretext of giving a chocolate the watchman asked her to come to his cottage and touched inappropriately. Juhi broke down in her mothers arms who consoled her. It did take Juhi some time to come back to her chirpy self and her mother made sure that she never let Juhi suffer anything like that again.

EIGHT

THE WAIT

Today Salma was excited as it was Diwali. Anoop had written to her that he will be back for Diwali. Yes you guessed it right. Salma and Anoop were college sweethearts. They were lucky enough unlike others to take their relationship to the next level. They got married even after facing opposition from salma's parents. Anoop's parents on the other hand were more welcoming to their union. The best part was she followed her faith,and also never lagged behind in following her husband's traditions.

Both of them had decided that once they plan to have children they will definitely grow in an interfaith environment. After college and getting married, Salma went on to do a corporate job and Anoop like his father and grandfather joined the army. It was tough staying away from each other immediately after marriage,but both of them were aware of what they were getting into. With distance their love grew even stronger.

Their source of communication were letters and calls. Anoop on completing the training was posted in North eastern states where the condition was hostile.He executed many coveted operations in that area and brought the situation under control.As days went by the letters and calls became sparse.

One fine day Salma received a letter from Anoop that he is coming back for Diwali. Salma couldn't be more ecstatic. Just days to go for Diwali Salma got busy with the preparations. Preparing his choice of sweets, decorating the house to his taste. Finally it was Diwali the day when Lord Rama returned back to Ayodhya, and it is said that the entire place was lit up with oil lamps to welcome Lord Rama.Like wise Salma had decorated every nook and corner of the house with oil lamps for her Anoop.

She dressed up in her finest clothes maroon, Anoop loved her in Maroon. She was decked up in the finest of jewels to welcome her husband for whom she had been waiting desperately. The firecrackers had started bursting in the night sky. She could hear the entire area doused in the festivities. The playful voices of children. The rummy games of uncles. The chit chat gossip of aunties. The wafting smells of delicacies amidst all this chaos her eyes were only looking for Anoop and her ears only waiting to hear his voice.

Hours went by until it was almost midnight. She waited and waited. Slowly she dragged herself to her room and undressed herself and wept herself to sleep. There hung on the wall of her bedroom was Anoop's well framed photo garlanded.Anoop was martyred three years ago in an ambush. Her last letter to Salma was three years ago when he was supposed to come home for Diwali. But he didn't. He had to tend to an important mission, which turned out to be his last,as he never saw the light of day. He was honoured with the highest award for sacrificing his life and serving his nation. Salma on the other hand never got out of the shock and still thinks that Anoop will return one day. So every Diwali she waits and waits for him to return.

NINE

A SECOND CHANCE

    Sitting at the cafe table Raima was damn nervous. It's not that she was on date for the first time. At the age of 48 with two married sons. She was quite content with life,but after her husband's untimely demise, Raima missed him. Somewhere down the line she had accepted her fate and moved on. But the cosmos seemed to have other plans for Raima. During the wedding of her second son she chanced upon to meet his Boss almost in his 50's. Mr.Marcus. He seemed to be a charming man and took an instant liking for Raima. At first Raima didn't pay much heed to him,but couldn't ignore him either. Marcus on the other hand seemed an adamant man, who somehow got his hand on Raima's cell number . Now just for the record Raima was not a techno freak. She managed a cell phone only because of her sons. So when Marcus called

Raima, Raima being unaware, picked up the call.
Raima: hello!
Marcus: Hello....Raima? This is Marcus here.
Raima: oh! Hello Mr.Marcus ..How are You?

Marcus: Please call me Marcus. I'm fine ...How are you? I have called you for something important.

Raima: Yes i'm good Mr Marcus......I mean Marcus... What is it? I hope nothing serious.

Marcus: No not really.... But its kind of serious to me....I want to ask you out on a date.

Raima: Marcus aren't we too old to date?

Marcus: I don't see a law on dating...or any age criteria. Are you aware of something like that?

Raima(smiling): But why would you want to go out on a date with me?

Marcus: Why do women ask such questions? When they know if a guy asks her out on a date it's obvious he likes her.

Raima: Just wanted to make sure.

Marcus : So What do you say ?

Raima Just a casual date!! Nothing more nothing less

Marcus: Don't worry i get into the women's pants only on the second or third date.

Raima : So you are expecting a third date?

Marcus: Why is that a crime?

Raima: No not at all....Fine then Sunday 10:30 let's have a date over brunch.

So as it turned out Raima was waiting for Marcus and to Raima's surprise Marcus turned up with some beautiful flowers to make an impression on his date. Raima was quite impressed. They exchanged pleasantries and settled down to order.

Marcus: What would you like to have?

Raima: Chicken in white sauce with assorted veggies and garlic bread on the side and one kiwi mojito.

Marcus: Wow! great choice and great appetite too. I will have the same.

Once the order was placed they started their conversation and Marcus got down straight to the point.

Marcus: See Raima I like you. I'm divorced and never thought of settling down again. But at your son's wedding everything changed. I thought I could at least give it a try.

Raima: I'm a widow and 48 years old. My kids are married and have you ever thought about what society might say.

Marcus: Wow!!! Calm down Raima don't jump the wagon. Let's get to know each other if things workout then good or else we can at least be friends.

Raima: I don't think it's a good idea.

Marcus: Cumon...Don't be such a baby. Think about it, everyone needs a companion.

Raima: I don't need anybody's support.

Marcus: I'm not trying to support you or make you dependent on me. All I'm saying is I want to accompany you on the remaining journey of our life. Think about it.

Raima: I don't think so.

After their brunch they cordially parted. Promising each other they will inform incase they changed their minds. weeks went by and one fine day Raima gathered up some courage and called Marcus

Raima: Hello Marcus

Marcus: Hello Raima how are you?? I was expecting your call.

Raima: Is it?

Marcus: Yes, I was waiting for you.

Raima: I thought about what you said about companionship and all.

Marcus:.. And??

Raima: I think we can give it a try at least.

Marcus: I'm glad to hear that. You can't imagine my happiness.

Once Raima agreed they both started meeting often. Going for movies, visiting art galleries, attending theatre, cooking together or just taking a walk. They would have conversations on old classical songs at length. They had so much in common from books, to old records. Raima seemed to have found a perfect match in Marcus after five decades of her life. Enjoying each moment like a teenager. One night when they were binge watching old movies. Marcus leaned close to her and pecked her on her lips. Something got into Raima and she pulled Marcus closer to her and kissed him passionately. The kisses went on to passionate love making. On waking up in the morning Raima was found crying

Marcus: Hey what happened? Did I hurt you? Was I rough on you last night?

Raima:(still crying): .No, it was really passionate,tender and cared for i have felt in years.

Marcus: Then why are you crying. You are scaring me Raima.

Raima: I have sinned. Im old.. I'm not supposed to do all this. The way we feel for each other is a crime.

Marcus: (holding raima in his arm): It's not a crime. We are just two people who happen to like each other and this is just a next phase in our relationship. We have done nothing wrong. Stop blaming yourself for nothing.

Raima: Are you sure? We are not commiting a crime.?

Marcus: No, dear we are not.

As days went by Marcus and Raima could be seen completely in love. At 50 they are in a live-in relationship, and enjoying the remainder of their life's journey with the best soul mate they could ever find.

TEN

THE STORY TELLER

"You know children when I moved to Bombay, now Mumbai in my youth in search of a better life. I used to do odd jobs to pay for my college. We used to sell photos of Gods and Goddesses at the dock to travellers coming in from foreign lands, by telling them various stories. Like lord shiva is the God of destruction if you don't buy ,the trip will be full of hurdles for you. Or in case of Goddess Lakshmi she will bring wealth and prosperity to you. And the "firangis" used to buy those photos for 10 rupees. It was equivalent to 1000 of today"

Well to all you readers that's my grandpa yes. He has many stories to tell. He never gets tired of them. He travelled around the world before he married my grandma. But stories of his journey are what he is popular for. One famous affair of his with a Russian traveller was his favourite.. To which my grandma always use to get irritated. They are an adorable couple. I remember him telling me about the Russian woman, when I fell in love with my wife.

"You know "beta" she was white as milk and her lips red as a rose. She was here to discover India and its culture. She had the most softest of hands. She spoke in broken english. But our hearts understood us in ways I can't imagine. She taught me how to kiss, she was my first kiss.. With her blonde hair she looked like an angel ascended from the heavens. The best part the sex, it was awesome."

We always giggled at this story. For he still had that Russian woman's picture in black and white in his old trunk. I guess that's what true love feels like. I guess he would have married her but I she was a traveller and things didn't work out. I never asked either.

My grandpa always used to sit at his favourite place on the porch facing the garden reading his newspaper on his rocking chair.

Once I introduced him to the new technology of mobile phones. He was surprised and opened another pandora.

"You know in my days talking on the phone was a privilege. We used telegrams more.The indian postal service has stopped it now. It was like the instant messaging service of today. The worst part about telegram was that everyone feared it would be bad news, especially a death of a loved one. But now such superstitious beliefs are far behind. Your generation is always on the phone. From movies to calls, to make up to breakup, everything has become instant ,but I miss the charm of the old world"

That's how my grandpa is: you say something or do something. He has a story to tell you. He was a good conversationalist. He could talk about anything and everything. Most of my life was spent listening to his stories. How he would pluck mangoes from his neighbour's orchard or how he would fly his kite to how he would sell liquor illegally just for the extra bucks. The most I enjoyed is the various thing he has eaten which I can't even imagine.

"When I travelled to south Africa I tasted crocodile meat. I tell you it tastes similar to chicken meat. Peacock is a beautiful bird but I tell you it's meat is even more succulent. Fried insects and butterflies to starfish. To snakes you name them I have eaten them. I didn't enjoy kangaroo meat though as it was too rubbery. But dog meat pickles are fantastic"

Now if you just had something to eat before this story , there is a hundred percent chance that you might end up vomiting, if not then you might lose an appetite for the rest of the day. That's how grandpa was a complete entertainer. You just couldn't ignore him.

One evening I was returning back from work and saw grandpa dozed off on his rocking chair. But something seemed different. He was not snoring. I went closer only to realise my story teller has ended his book of stories. I lost him that day but he will be remembered for his lovely stories and the wonderful life he led.

ELEVEN
THE PROMISE

Sitting beside his fathers death bed. Sobbing at the thought of losing him, Ananth was terrified. His father was everything for him. His idol, his guide, his mentor. It was after independence that the law to abolish the zamindari system came into being in 1950. Ananth's father had lost huge acres of land to this law. This setback was too big for him which had gotten him severely sick. He took to drinking and eventually ended up getting tuberculosis. With very less or nothing in hand it was getting difficult to treat him. Ananth was still in college. It was the darkest night for Ananth. As he remembered being called by his father to his room.

Ananth: baba you need anything??

Father: No,come sit beside me. I want to tell you something.

Ananth gets close to the bed and sits.

Father: I have never asked you for anything my son.But i need a favour from you now.

Ananth: Anything baba.

Father: Promise me whatever land we have lost you will get it back. It's our ancestors, nobody can take that away from us.

Ananth: ok baba I promise .I will get it all back.

The next day the sky came shattering down on Ananth his baba was gone. He was inconsolable. But he had to get on as he had to lead his mother and younger brother out of this misery. He took up a job at a glass factory and spent each and every penny on his mother and younger brother. By day he was in college by night he was working .He hardly slept. His hard work didn't go unnoticed by his boss. Who after Ananth's graduation offered him a job in the gulf. He was delighted at this gesture. His mother was sceptical yet gave her blessings to pursue his career. He was sent as manager for the company's gulf branch in Bahrain. The gulf back in the 1970's was not that developed . The businessmen there were always in search of good English and Hindi speaking people. As to bridge the communication gap.

Ananth had an upper hand on both his education and language sector. So it was a bonus point for Ananth. It was unbelievable as he used to send back ten thousand rupees to his family every month. It was a huge amount as even the biggest of the biggest officers in India did not earn that much in those days. When he returned back, as promised to his father he bought back all the land which was distributed to others under the zamindari abolition act. He rebuilt his house. It was so huge with nine rooms on the ground floor and seven rooms on the upper floor. It was a spectacular view in the village. People envied Ananth. To his surprise one of the people who despised him was his own younger brother Ravi.

Ananth loved him like his own son. But Ravi on the other hand hated him. Entire village including his mother taunted him for not being as capable as his brother. He was always overshadowed by Ananth and his abilities.As time went by Ananth rose financially he would send huge amounts home and never ask what they did with it. Ananth who worked for almost ten years in Bahrain now wanted to return home,settle down and start a family. Ananth married at his own will to someone he had met back in Bahrain. Her name was Ruksana Indian but muslim. His mother and brother were extremely furious when he bought Ruksana home.

Mother: How could you marry a muslim?

Ananth: Mom I love her and she loves me and I thought you would understand your son.

Mother: Even if I do have you ever thought what will people say.? We won't be able to show our faces to any of our relatives.

Ravi: I will not accept a meat eater as my sister in law.

Ananth was so furious and slapped Ravi. In anger Ravi returned the slap with a punch and a hussle broke. Somehow the mother broke them apart and blamed it on the new bride.

Mother: The moment she stepped into the house,she made you brothers fight.God knows what all bad luck she is going to bring.

Ananth was so upset with his family. He worked hard all his life just for his mother and brother and asked nothing in return. Now for once he thought of his happiness and they were spewing venom on his wife. He decided to leave his mother and brother for ever and never return. The next morning when he packed and was about to leave. His mother asked him the most daunting thing.

Mother: Before you leave, sign these papers.

Ananth: Maa what is this?

Mother: Property papers. It is mentioned in this that you are handing over the house and land to your brother Ravi and that you have no right or claim on it.

Ananth Without a second thought, signed the papers.

Mother: Promise me you will return only when you leave this girl

Ananth:Maa I promise I will never return.

As he left his house the one he bulit,the roof of the house came crashing down damaging a bit of the foundation of the house. Ananth's heart was completely shattered as he looked one last time at that place which he built with his own sweat and blood. As his car moved away he could see only his house and reminisce about his father

TWELVE
THE DECISION

"I want an abortion" said Bina slowly to her husband Vikram.

Vikram was stunned at first. They had been married for three years and the pressure to have children was building up from the both sides of the family. Vikram composed himself and said, "Lets have this one at least we can keep our families calm for sometime."

"To keep the families calm do you want me to sacrifice my life and have no say to decide what to do with my body?. I can't have a child now with the new promotion and responsibilities I can't take a back seat. It's my body and nobody should have a say in it. Let me manage this position for two years and then we can plan for a baby." said Bina.

"I'm not asking you to compromise on anything, but now it's the right time. I think we should start a family, you know how much I love kids." Vikram said

"I know you love kids so do I. I'm not denying but I'm just asking for more time." said Bina.

"I don't think more time is required. We can have the kid and then you can pursue your career again and besides I'm earning well enough even if you don't work it won't make a difference. So you stay home and take care of the baby and I will earn" said vikram

"It makes a difference to me vikram. I worked my ass off for this job. I can't just give it all up for something that has not even come into this world yet." said bina

"It's already in this world, in your womb" vikram said.

Bina kept quiet for a while. She pulled a piece of paper out of her bag and handed it to vikram. He was shocked to see the paper.

"Appointment for abortion? Have you gone insane bina. You didn't even bother to ask me, you went ahead and decided to abort. Don't forget it's my child too."

"You just have to sign it. If it was not required I wouldn't have let you know I would have done it anyway. As a woman I have the right to choose if I want the baby or not." said Bina.

Out of anger Vikram signed it and threw the paper on the floor. Bina picked it up and kept it in her bag. The dinner went without any conversation. The night wouldn't let them sleep. Both were wide awake. Their thoughts and anxiety filled their room. Suddenly breaking the silence of the night Vikram said,

"Bina I think you shouldn't compromise with your career. I have seen you work really hard. Although I love kids but I love you even more. I don't want you to suffer. So whatever your decision I will be with you. I know as a woman it must be hard for you too, to take such a drastic step. But as your husband I do understand. I love you bina and I only want you to be happy. That's all. I was getting succumbed to parental pressure. But it's our life and I think we should decide for ourselves and our family life. Tomorrow I will accompany you to the the clinic"

When Bina heard all this she had tears in her eyes. As she seemed to have different thoughts in her mind. She didn't utter a word. But her tears said it all. They both held each other in their arms, hugged each other tightly and slept. Bina's silence spoke louder than words.

About The Author

Vini Kunhappan was born in Dubai U.A.E. She is the daughter of a Malayali father and Maharashtrian mother. Her interest in writing was initiated at an early age by her mother and storytelling was something she picked up from her father. Her early childhood was spent in the laps of the desert country. She completed her basic education from Progressive English School, Sharjah U.A.E. She graduated in botany from Icles Motilal Jhunjhunwala college Navi Mumbai. She currently resides in Navi Mumbai where she works as a primary teacher. Like her writing, teaching is something she is equally passionate about. Since she was born and raised in a mixed culture, her stories are also a reflection of the same. She is also one of the authors for Out of my box and Dear Ma. She is a certified content writer. She is also a part of the WriteFluence community where

ABOUT THE AUTHOR

you can find her poems and blogs. One of her blogs was also selected by WriteFluence for their podcast which is available on Spotify. She also has her own blog Vini's adda (vinik0404@wordpress.com) where she writes her mind out. You can also find her write ups on her instagram page @victoriousvini. When she is not writing or teaching, she usually enjoys a good book accompanied by a hot cup of chai.

About WriteFluence

WriteFluence is an innovative literary community featuring worthy authors and showcasing their talent. WriteFluence provides literary services such as publishing, book editing, proofreading, book designing, author branding and book promotions.

Visit us now at **https://writefluence.in**
OR
Follow us on Instagram/Facebook/Twitter
@writefluence

Books published by WriteFluence:

Wafting Earthy is a compilation of the winning short stories of the international premier league short-story contest PenFuenza, organized by WriteFluence. The book consists of 31 literary pieces written by prolific writers in different genres and based on the theme of 'Fragrances' and were selected from a whopping 142 submissions that had been received from all over the world for the contest. PenFluenza, described as one of the most comprehensive creative writing contests by several online entities was indeed structured that way to make sure the best of writers could be brought together under one book cover. The contest had a theme, a specific word limit and a very proficient jury.

In January 2021 WriteFluence announced their very first exclusively-for-women-writers story-writing contest FemmeFluenza and received a whopping 79 entries in a span of just a month!

Out of my BOX is a collection of brilliant plots woven alongside the theme of celebrating womanhood and surviving through various challenges it brings along.

Spent is a curated collection of winning poems from amongst 200+ submissions received on this poetry writing prompt based on the theme of Erotica; contest held by WriteFluence from December 2020 - January 2021.

Dear Ma, is a compilation of beautiful letters written by 19 writers to their mothers to celebrate the occasion of International Mother's Day, 2021!

www.ingramcontent.com/pod-product-compliance
Lightning Source LLC
LaVergne TN
LVHW021738060526
838200LV00052B/3353